Farmyard Tales

Scarecrow's Secret

Heather Amery

Illustrated by Stephen Cartwright

Adapted by Anna Milbourne

Reading consultant: Alison Kelly

Find the duck on every double page.

This story is about
Apple Tree Farm,

Mrs. Boot
the farmer,

Sam,

Poppy,

Mr. Boot,

Whiskers

and a
scarecrow.

Sam and Poppy were helping on the farm.

They collected some eggs.

Mr. Boot was in
the barn.

"What's that?"
asked Sam.

"You'll soon see,"
said Mr. Boot.

"Please can you get
my old coat?"

They brought the coat.

"I know what it is now,"
said Sam. "A scarecrow!"

They dressed the
scarecrow.

Poppy helped carry
the scarecrow outside.

Sam helped dig a hole.

They stood Mr. Straw
up in it.

"I bet he'll scare off all the crows," said Poppy.

The next day, they
came back.

There were no birds
at all.

They looked at Farmer
Dray's scarecrow.

Birds were eating all the corn in his field.

Why was Mr. Straw
so good?

"He looks as if he's
moving," said Poppy.

"Let's go and see."

They crept across
the field.

Mr. Straw's coat was twitching.

They opened the coat
and found...

Whiskers had two
new kittens.

So that was the
scarecrow's secret!

PUZZLES

Puzzle 1

Put the pictures in the right order to make a scarecrow.

A

B

C

D

E

Puzzle 2

What did Mr. Boot use to make the scarecrow?

coat

carrots

hat

eggs

socks

straw

What was Farmer Dray's
scarecrow made from?

coat   sticks

hat   straw

black   bucket
bag

25

Puzzle 3

Choose the right sentence
for each picture.

A

They washed the scarecrow.
They dressed the scarecrow.

B

They crept across the field.
They crept across the moon.

Puzzle 4

Spot five differences between these two pictures.

Answers to puzzles

Puzzle 1

1B

2E

3C

4A

5D

Puzzle 2

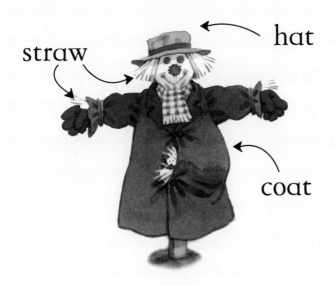

hat

straw

coat

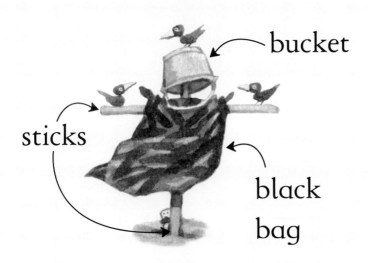

bucket

sticks

black
bag

Puzzle 3

A

They <u>dressed</u> the scarecrow.

B

They crept across the <u>field</u>.

Puzzle 4

Designed by Laura Nelson
Series editor: Lesley Sims
Series designer: Russell Punter
Digital manipulation by John Russell
and Nick Wakeford

This edition first published in 2015 by Usborne Publishing Ltd.,
Usborne House, 83-85 Saffron Hill, London EC1N 8RT, England.
www.usborne.com Copyright © 2015, 1990 Usborne Publishing Ltd.